WHEN THE
HORSES RIDE BY

CHILDREN IN THE TIMES OF WAR

POEMS BY **ELOISE GREENFIELD**

ILLUSTRATIONS BY **JAN SPIVEY GILCHRIST**

LEE & LOW BOOKS INC. • NEW YORK

HELPING CHILDREN COPE: RESOURCES FOR EDUCATORS, PARENTS, AND CAREGIVERS

Bank Street College of Education
  streetcat.bnkst.edu/html/resources.html

National Association of School Psychologists
  nasponline.org/NEAT/helpingchildrencope.html

National Mental Health Association
  nmha.org/reassurance/childrenDealwithWar.cfm

U.S. Department of Health & Human Services/National Child Care Information Center
  nccic.org/poptopics/cope.html

U.S. Department of Health & Human Services/National Mental Health Information Center
  mentalhealth.samhsa.gov/cmhs/TraumaticEvents/teachers.asp

U.S. Department of State
  state.gov/m/dghr/flo/c8894.htm

Thanks to Beth Nichols of the Flossmoor Public Library, Youth Division, Flossmoor, Illinois, for help with the extensive research for this book. —J.S.G.

Grateful acknowledgment is made to Alfred A. Knopf for permission to reprint the excerpt from "Dreams" from THE COLLECTED POEMS OF LANGSTON HUGHES by Langston Hughes, copyright © 1994 by The Estate of Langston Hughes. Used by permission of Alfred A. Knopf, a division of Random House, Inc.

Text copyright © 2006 by Eloise Greenfield
Illustrations copyright © 2006 by Jan Spivey Gilchrist

LEE & LOW BOOKS Inc., 95 Madison Avenue,
New York, NY 10016   leeandlow.com

Manufactured in China

Book design by Tania Garcia
Book production by The Kids at Our House

The text is set in Worcester Round
The illustrations are rendered in mixed-media collage

10 9 8 7 6 5 4 3 2 1
First Edition

Library of Congress Cataloging-in-Publication Data

Greenfield, Eloise.
  When the horses ride by : children in the times of war / poems by Eloise Greenfield ; illustrations by Jan Spivey Gilchrist.— 1st ed.
      p. cm.
  Summary: "Collection of poems about children around the world, focusing on the children's perceptions of war and how the turmoil of war affects their lives. An author's note provides additional context"—Provided by publisher.
  ISBN-13: 978-1-58430-249-0
  ISBN-10: 1-58430-249-6
1. Children and war—Juvenile poetry. 2. Children's poetry, American. 3. War—Juvenile poetry. I. Gilchrist, Jan Spivey. II. Title.
PS3557.R39416W47 2006
811'.54—dc22   2005015393

To the children of the world —*E.G.*

For the beautiful, powerful, and courageous children of the world.
You are far more than dolls and toy trucks; you are real people only
smaller. Know that we are here to love you, listen to you, respect
you, and protect you. Be forever empowered and be prepared
for the next time the horses ride by. —*J.S.G.*

Hold fast to dreams

For if dreams die

Life is a broken-winged bird

That cannot fly.

Langston Hughes, from "Dreams"

I THINK I KNOW

I think I know what war
is all about.
Listen:
This one was mad at that one,
and that one was angry, too.
Then the others said,
"Since you two are mad,
we're going to be mad at you."
Now, everyone's mad
at somebody else,
and everyone wants to be right.
And how to decide
who the winner is?
They fight.

WE ARE HELPERS

We tend the farm,
help to make the food grow.
Somewhere there is fighting,
but we are here, helping the sun
and the rain and the rich earth
bring forth the plants of life.

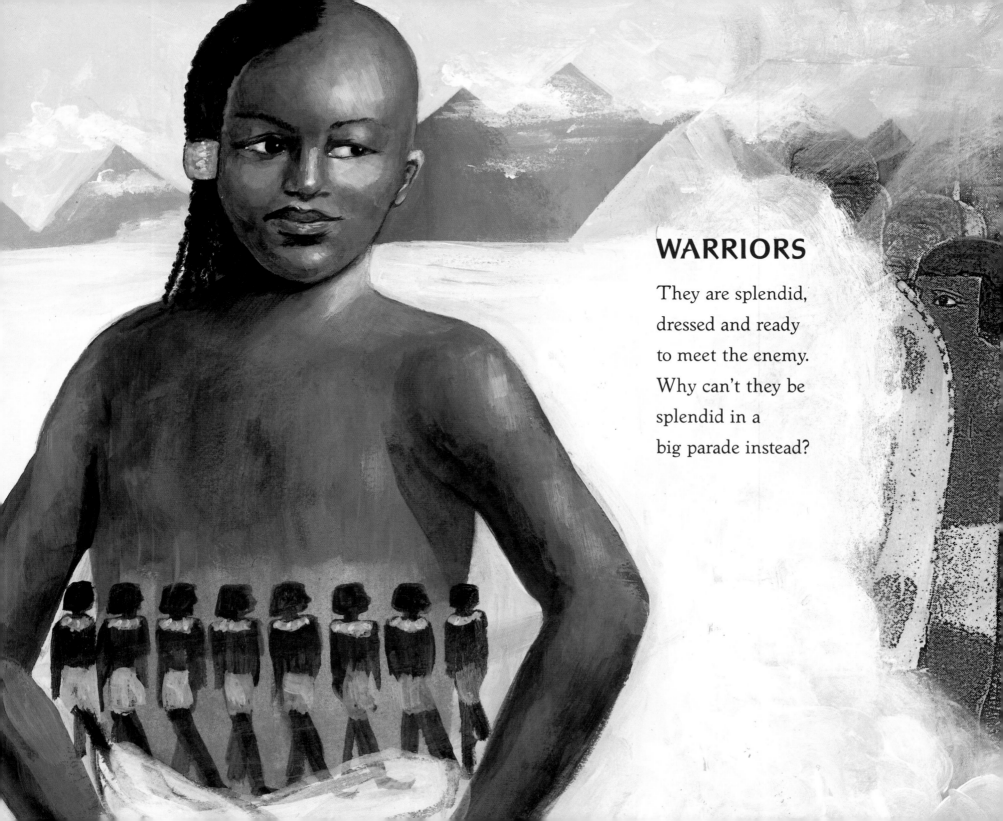

WARRIORS

They are splendid,
dressed and ready
to meet the enemy.
Why can't they be
splendid in a
big parade instead?

A DIFFERENT LAND

The wars came and pushed us
from the land of our ancestors.
We are covered by sadness.
But we take with us
memories of our ancestors,
and we will make this new land
ours.

PAPA

My papa came home today.
He kissed us and held us,
then closed his eyes
and sat and sat in silence.
But we will wait, Papa.
We will wait for you to rest
from the war.

WISH

From my house, high in the hills,
I send a wish.
If I could make magic,
I would throw handfuls
of golden dust,
like a million tiny magnets,
over the hills and over the valleys,
to bring all the fathers home.

WHEN THE HORSES RIDE BY

When the horses ride by,
with men on their backs,
we pretend they're going
anyplace, but war.
We tell each other stories:

They're on their way
to save somebody lost in a howling
storm, to help somebody dig a well,
build a house, build a barn.
The horses ride by,
on their way to anyplace,
but war.

A CHILD LIKE ME

Far away, on the other side of the world,
there is a child like me, head full
of scary thoughts,
heart full of wanting.
If we laugh, our laughter will meet
in the middle of the ocean, and we
will be friends.

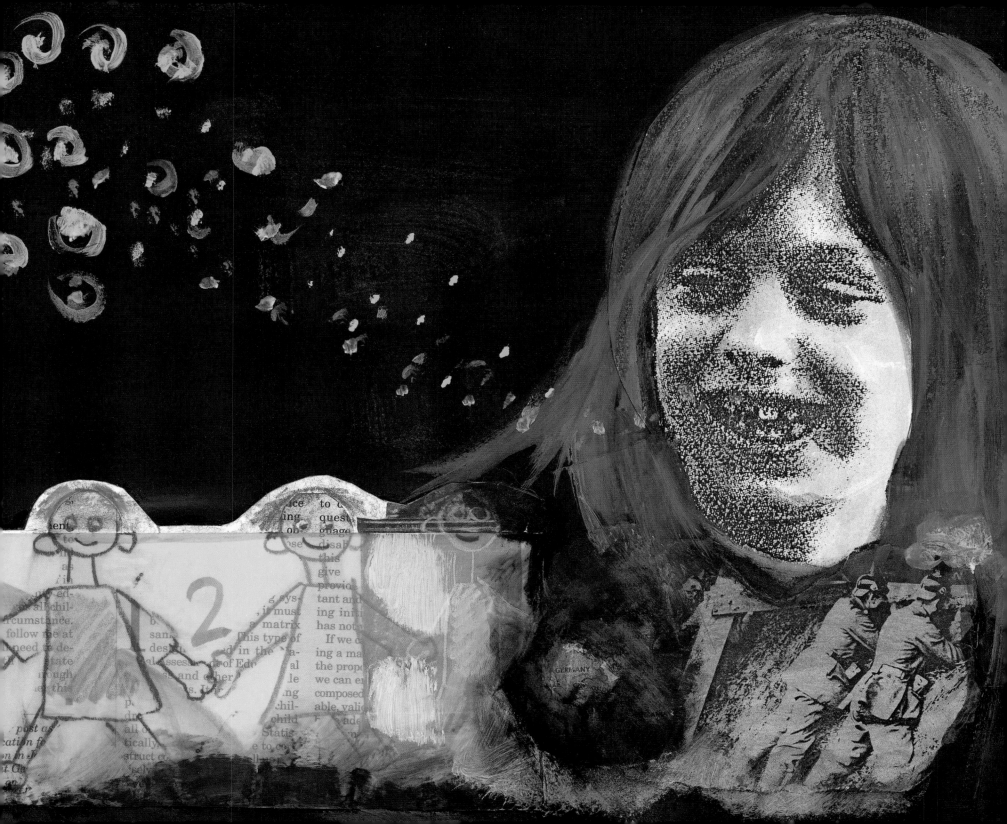

THE END OF THE WAR

The World

The people are set free,
they are prisoners no more,
their dreams of home
at last come true.
This is the end of war.

U.S.A.

"The war is over!"
The newsboy yells it, standing
at the corner, waving his papers,
so people will buy. They do,
and they hug their friends
and others, too. Some cry for joy,
some jump. Some shout the words,
some whisper, "The war is over,
it's over."

GREAT-GRANDMOTHER

Our great-grandmother takes care of us,
and we take care of her. When she's tired,
we rub her hands, sing to her,
are quiet when she wants to sleep.
But she's the one we lean on,
when trouble comes.

TOMORROW

The sirens are screaming,
"Hide! Hide!"
I run with my uncle
to our safe place
and hide inside
myself.
My song is there.
I sing it silently,
Oh, sweet warm air
has come again.
It brings new grass, new sky.
Tomorrow, I will sing it loud
and dance in the streets.

I SEE MR. MANDELA

He is at the microphone. I am in the crowd,
watching with my mother. We cheer.
"At last he is free," my mother says.
"They have held him in prison
because he loved freedom for all."
Someone begins a freedom song.
It sweeps through the crowd.
I, who know only some of the words,
sing them. My mother sings through her tears
for those who have died in the war.
We dance a dance of freedom, lifting our knees,
left, right, left, right. The dance and the song
tell of our strength. On the stage,
Mr. Mandela sings with us. He is strong.
He is home. He is ours.

I IMAGINE

I try to imagine that there is no war,
that trouble and hatred will hurt me no more.
I draw a picture of my land
in peace, but then, like storms of sand,
war swirls and flies and stings
and tries to snatch my precious picture
from my hand.
But I hold on. I hold on
to dreams.

VOICES

I hear their voices
mixing with the sounds of war.
Too much noise, almost
drowning out their words,
drowning out my thoughts.
Almost.

WHEREVER WE ARE

Wherever we are,
we search for a place
to be unafraid.
Wherever we are.

TOYS

Still, we play.
Our toys take us
to happy places.
We bounce the balls,
beat the drum,
make sweet music
for the world to hear.

STILL

Still, we plan and we pray.
We are surrounded by love,
taking us through
the danger days.
We give to the world,
still,
our wonder, our wisdom,
our laughter, our hope.
We are the children.
We are the children . . .
. . . still.

A NOTE FROM THE AUTHOR

Dear Children,

Wars have occurred throughout history, in all parts of the world. War is not pretty. It causes suffering. Somehow, though, in spite of this, people find a way to see the beauty in life. Grown-ups see it, especially in the love they have for children. It is the kind of love that gives parents, grandparents, aunts, and uncles a reason not to give up in difficult times. Like the children in this book, you can find in this love, and in the beauty of plants and song and play and imagination, a way to hold on to dreams and hope.

As I was writing this book, I had a wish: that each one of you who reads these poems, or hears them, will understand what is possible for you, if you never let go of your dreams.

Eloise Greenfield

Poems in this book represent the following historical periods and events.

WE ARE HELPERS: Ancient China*

WARRIORS: Ancient Egypt*

A DIFFERENT LAND: Displacement of Native Americans during U. S. western expansion, 1700s–1800s

PAPA: American Revolution, 1775–1783

WISH: South American wars of independence, 1810–1828

WHEN THE HORSES RIDE BY: American Civil War, 1861–1865

A CHILD LIKE ME: World War I, 1914–1918

THE END OF THE WAR: World War II, 1939–1945

GREAT-GRANDMOTHER: Vietnam War, 1954–1975

TOMORROW: South African protests against apartheid, 1950s–1990

I SEE MR. MANDELA: Celebration of Nelson Mandela's release from prison, 1990

I IMAGINE: Iraq War (second Gulf War), 2003–

*Historians generally agree that ancient times existed until about the sixth century, although the specific time period for each civilization is different. Some dates may vary slightly from those listed due to discrepancies among sources.